TREVOR

TREVOR

Text and Illustrations by

JAMES LECESNE

Seven Stories Press

NEW YORK

A Seven Stories Press First Edition

Seven Stories Press
140 Watts Street
New York, NY 10013
www.sevenstories.com

College professors may order examination copies of Seven Stories Press titles for a free six-month trial period. To order, visit http://www.sevenstories.com/ textbook or send a fax on school letterhead to (212) 226-1411.

Library of Congress Cataloging-in-Publication Data

Lecesne, James.
   Trevor / James Lecesne. -- 1st ed.
      p. cm.
Summary: Bullied at school, dumped by his friends, and pressured at home, an artistic teenager struggling with his sexuality and identity makes a desperate attempt to end his loneliness.
   Includes bibliographical references (p.).
   ISBN 978-1-60980-420-6 (hardback) -- ISBN 1-60980-420-1 (hardback)
   [1. Sexual orientation--Fiction. 2. Sex role--Fiction. 3. Suicide--Fiction.] I. Title.
PZ7.L483Tr 2012
[Fic]--dc23
                                                 2012016377

Book design by Jon Gilbert

Printed in the USA

9 8 7 6 5 4 3 2 1

This book is dedicated to the memory of

Randy Stone

cofounder of The Trevor Project

CONTENTS

Trevor.. 9

Afterword 89

Acknowledgments.....................97

Resource Guide.......................101

About The Trevor Project 107

About the Author....................109

ONE

There I was, lying on the front lawn in plain sight with a knife in my back. Actually that was the effect I was going for, and to be perfectly honest, I think it looked pretty good—from the street. I had gone to a lot of trouble in order to create the illusion that I'd been murdered. First, I borrowed Mom's kitchen knife (the big one) and planted it firmly in the dirt. Then I positioned my body so that it looked to the people who happened to be driving by in their cars that I'd been stabbed to death. The fact that Dad was nonchalantly mowing the lawn made the whole thing seem (in my opinion) even more macabre. Imagine that you are driving past a typical suburban house on a typical suburban street in a typical suburban town somewhere in America at the beginning of the twenty-first century. A guy is mowing his lawn. You happen to turn your head and catch sight of this kid—thirteen years old, brown hair, wearing a t-shirt, jeans, and running shoes. He's lying on the grass with a knife stuck in his back. Horrors! What do you do? Do you turn your head away and pretend you didn't see it? Call 911? Stop and point out to the guy who is mowing the lawn that his kid appears to be dead? Do you stop the car, jump out, and administer mouth-to-mouth resuscitation? What?

These are a few of the questions I pondered while lying there trying to make it look like I wasn't breathing by keeping my chest and stomach perfectly still. It's hard to do, but I had been practicing this for years and eventually I developed a technique to simulate deadness. I can fool trained paramedics, which I did once when I was in seventh grade (the trained paramedic was my cousin Sara, but still). Anyway, I was doing a pretty good job of being a murder victim when I heard my Dad yell over the sound of the mower.

"WHAT?"

"MY KITCHEN KNIFE," Mom yelled back from the porch where she was standing. "HAVE YOU SEEN IT? THE BIG ONE?"

Dad did not reply, but I imagine that by this time Mom had spotted me lying there in plain sight along with her knife. I opened one eye just enough to see her marching across the front lawn. She was coming toward me, and she did not look happy. I'd say, based on her facial expression and body language, exasperation would be a more fitting description of her mental state. The fact that she was wearing an apron made me deduce that she had been in the middle of cooking dinner and then realized that her knife (the big one) was missing. After looking high and low, the logical next step would have been to ask Dad if he'd taken it from the kitchen. He is always using her kitchen utensils for inappropriate household activities like cutting tree branches or unscrewing something on his car. Once she

spotted me, I figured that I'd be receiving a good talking-to, so I shut my eyes and braced myself for her verbal onslaught.

Let me just say that Mom has never been my best audience. Ever. She has always been very busy with either housework or her job. As she often reminds me, she doesn't have the time or the energy for my "shenanigans" and she wishes to God that I would find something constructive to do with my time, something other than sitting in my room doodling for hours or lying on the front lawn pretending to be dead. What about baseball, she has asked me on more than one occasion. "Would it kill you to go over and ask that gang of boys if they needed an extra outfielder or something?" She didn't understand that in fact I *was* being constructive. I had gone to a lot of trouble in order to create the effect of my own murder on the front lawn, but unfortunately, due to her position, it was lost on her. I was really doing it for the benefit of the random people who were passing by our house. From the other angle, it must have looked as though I'd fallen asleep on the front lawn with the knife stuck in the grass beside me. I doubt she would have enjoyed having the whole thing explained to her, so I kept my mouth shut and kept on pretending to be dead. Knowing Mom, she probably was able to figure out what I was up to and just wasn't that impressed.

In any case, she reached down and quickly snatched the

knife from the lawn. Then she wheeled herself around and headed back toward the house without a word. She didn't even bother to yell at me. Maybe she thought I was doing this as a ploy to get attention, but I was just trying to keep myself entertained. It's fun to be pretend-dead and then lie there as the world goes on without you. In my opinion, this is a much better use of my time than playing baseball.

The mower started up again, but I could hear Dad's voice shouting over the sound of the revving motor.

"TREVOR," he yelled. "GET UP. I HAVE TO FINISH THE LAWN AND YOU'RE IN THE WAY . . . TREVOR!"

TWO

I don't want to give you the impression that Mom and Dad are uncaring people who are insensitive to my needs; they are merely busy. Mom works as an administrator processing applications for insurance claims—or something like that—at the local hospital. Dad is a regional manager for a company that distributes products designed to make things that stick, like tape and industrial-strength glue. As an artist, I am not exactly inspired by the type of work they do, but I totally appreciate the fact that ever since I can remember they have kept a roof over my head and sent me to school fed and fully dressed. As their only child, I have always had pretty much everything I need. We are not rich by any means. I guess you could say that we are comfortably well off. Mom and Dad are tired at the end of the day—the result of their hard work—and they like to relax in the evening by parking themselves in front of the TV and watching some dumb game show or a televised talent contest in which people are pitted against one another until one of them wins a chance to be recognized by strangers in shopping malls across the country.

One night, while they were watching TV, I walked into the living room and fell dead to the floor. I held my breath a good long time. No response from them. That was when I decided that their ability to spontaneously respond to their environment (and me) had been compromised by the television. Unless I happened to be dancing with a star, I don't think they would notice me—and I have never danced with a star in my whole life.

Sometimes instead of hanging around in my room surfing the net, drawing, or just being ignored to death by my parents, I sneak out of the house and go over to Zac's house, which is just four blocks away. Zac and I have been friends since second grade, but now that we're in high school and we don't do kid stuff anymore, we have been working on more grown-up activities. For example, one night Zac asked me if I wanted to come over and check out his new microscope. I said yes, hopped on my bike, and went upstairs to his room without his parents knowing what was up. And wow! Let me tell you, we saw a lot of crazy activity through the eyepiece of that microscope. His sperm was amazing! Zac said that people used to think masturbating could cause a person to go totally deaf.

Apparently he had read all about this and, according to the Internet, it was something they told to young boys in order to get them to stop "abusing" themselves.

"I am no expert," I told Zac, "but I've never heard of a single case where someone went deaf due to masturbation."

"What'd you say?!" Zac asked, pretending to be deaf.

We had big laugh over that one.

Then things got ugly.

He asked me if I was planning to dress up for Halloween, and I told him that I was considering going as Lady Gaga.

"Why?" he asked, and I could tell that he disapproved of my idea.

I explained to him that Lady Gaga was (a) my absolute fave, (b) an icon, and (c) an original who knew how to

upend people's expectations of normalcy. He wasn't convinced, and announced that he was going to be a superhero for Halloween. He suggested that I join him, or at the very least consider something "less gay." I informed him that Lady Gaga was certainly not gay.

"You're missing the whole point," he told me.

Before he could say anything further, I jumped in: "No, Zac, *you're* missing the point. Because anyone who knows anything about Lady Gaga knows that she has had to overcome plenty of obstacles to become the artist that she is today. And in order to be myself and achieve my goals, I will have to do the same."

He rolled his eyes and said, "Whatever."

End of discussion.

After that I was even more determined than ever to be the most awesome, gender-bending version of Lady Gaga for Halloween. Mom dropped me at the mall, and with my birthday money, I purchased the following items:

> One full-body leotard (black): $14.95
>
> One wig (blond): $18.45
>
> One sequined cape (silver): $19.99
>
> One pair of oversize sunglasses (black): $8.00
>
> One pair of platform slouch boots (black): $27.99
>
> 2-lb bag of glitter (silver): $10.00
>
> TOTAL: $99.38

THREE

Last week in art history class, Mr. Livorgna explained to us how sometimes great art can be both a reaction to the politics of the moment and an enduring statement about the human condition. To prove his point, he pulled up some famous paintings on his laptop. He showed us a mostly black-and-white painting of crudely drawn people and animals—they all seemed to be suffering violently. A horse, a bull, a baby, and a person lying on the ground stretching out his hand for help. To us, it looked like a gruesome mess drawn by a fifth-grader. Mr. Livorgna explained that the artist was, in fact, Picasso and that gruesome was the whole point. *Guernica* (that's the name of the painting) was created to show the tragedies of war and the suffering it inflicts upon individuals, particularly innocent civilians. He said the work gained a monumental status right from the start, becoming famous and widely acclaimed when it was displayed around the world. Incidentally, he said, this tour helped bring the Spanish Civil War to the world's attention. Who knew that Spain even had a Civil War?

"Can you think of any other examples of how artists have brought about change through their work?" he asked us.

Silence.

I almost raised my hand to mention how Lady Gaga had famously worn a suit made entirely of meat in order to protest the fact that gays in the military had to keep their sexuality a secret or else be kicked out with a dishonorable discharge. But then I thought better of it. I didn't want everyone to think that I followed gay news. Besides I couldn't say for sure whether Lady Gaga's meat-suit media moment actually brought an end to the policy the army called "Don't Ask, Don't Tell." The fact that this policy existed for seventeen years but was overturned by Congress just a couple of months after she wore the suit wasn't proof of anything. Some people said that Lady Gaga was just an opportunist who was using the politics of the moment to further her career. Some said she was an activist. I wondered if Picasso had the same trouble with *Guernica*.

When no one could come up with any examples, Mr. Livorgna clicked on to the next image, and started to describe a painting entitled *La Mort de Marat*, which is French for *The Death of Marat*. The style of this painting was much more realistic and it depicted a man who had been stabbed in his bathtub while writing a letter. It was very dramatic, and the guy was obviously very dead. Little spurts of blood stained some sheets that spilled out of the tub; he was wearing a white turban and held a feather pen in his right hand, which had dropped dramatically to the floor at the moment of his murder. Mr. Livorgna told us that this was one of the most famous images of the French Revolution, and it referred to the assassination of a radical journalist named Jean-Paul Marat.

When I got home I Googled the image and read all about Monsieur Marat. Not only was he a journalist, but he was also a doctor, a statesman, and a great public speaker. I don't know why, but I became fascinated by this image and the story of how Jean-Paul had been killed in his bathtub by a French revolutionary named Charlotte Corday. Perhaps it reminded me that anything could happen to any one of us at any moment. Our lives could change—or end—with a moment's notice.

For my art history extra credit project I decided to recreate the scene from *La Mort de Marat*. An artist that Mr. Livorgna visually introduced us to the week before had inspired me. Her name was Cindy Sherman, and starting in the 1970s she began to make a name for herself by being photographed in the guises of random people. My plan was to take a picture of myself in the bath in the pose of poor old Marat, and then

maybe be discovered as the youngest artist of my generation. I got a hold of my mother's terry-cloth shower turban,
I found an old quill pen that I had purchased years ago when
I went to Philadelphia on a school trip to view the actual
Declaration of Independence, and I bought a packet of fake
blood from the Halloween section of the local card shop. I
was all set and super excited. After applying the blood to my
body and the sheet, I sat in the bathtub and tried to imagine

what it must have felt like to be murdered by a revolutionary who was brave (or crazy) enough to come to where I live and stab me in my bath.

Unfortunately, I was interrupted by the sound of my mother pulling back the shower curtain and then turning on the faucet. Before I knew what was happening, a steady stream of cold water had extinguished my French Revolutionary fantasy, and any chance of extra credit went swirling down the drain.

"Clean up this mess," said Mom, as she presented me with a wet sponge mop.

What Mom failed to understand was that, just like Lady Gaga, I refused to be discouraged from becoming an artist or expressing my true self in an artistic way. And just like Lady Gaga, I intended to change the world.

FOUR

"What's wrong?" Mom asked me.

I was pushing my breakfast burrito around on my plate, not exactly eating, but not exactly not eating either.

"Nothing," I told her.

She wasn't convinced.

"Why don't you invite Zac over after school and play a board game? Wouldn't that be fun?"

A board game? I haven't played a board game since I was in fourth grade. Sometimes Mom can be so retro. Hasn't she heard of computers? The Internet? Facebook?

"You mean, a *bored* game?" I asked her, without looking up from my plate.

Mom shook her head, downed the rest of her coffee, and went about her business. What I couldn't tell her was that Zac and I were no longer friends; he had stopped returning my calls, and when I passed him in the hallway at school, he kind of totally brushed me off. Finally I confronted him at his locker, saying, "What's up?"

He responded by looking around and saying in a voice that was louder than necessary: "Well, if it isn't Lady Gay-Gay."

As a result of that experience, I made a decision to expand my social horizons and accept an invitation to hang out with a gang of kids I hardly knew. Katie Quinn said it would be cool for me to join her and her posse after school because they were planning to hang out at the Quality Courts Motel, and another body wouldn't make any difference one way or the other.

"Cool," I said in response.

I didn't know what to expect, but what I discovered was that the motel hadn't actually been completed; it was just a construction site at the far end of town with a "COMING SOON" sign. We all scaled the fence, boys and girls together, and then once inside the structure, we checked the place out, wandering from floor to floor and calling to one another like idiots. Eventually, someone yelled that they'd found a few habitable rooms, and one of the guys declared that these rooms would be our new clubhouse until further notice.

Somehow I ended up alone in a room with Katie. Since we had nothing better to do and there was no place to sit, I suggested that we try to French-kiss. I told her that we could consider it a controlled experiment. To tell you the truth, I had no trouble controlling myself. I didn't feel anything. Maybe it was the fact that Katie has braces on her teeth, but I remember thinking: Is this what all the fuss is about? And what makes it French?

In any case, Katie and I made a date to try it again soon.

When I got home, Mom was in a state. Where had I been all this time? Why hadn't I answered my cell phone? Did I see the text messages she sent me? She sent me seven of them. Seven! She had been so worried that she was about to call the police. And what was the matter with my lips? Why were they so red and swollen?

When I explained to her that I had been kissing a girl, it was like the sun had broken through the clouds. Her face lit up, and she smiled as though she had just been awarded an all-expenses paid Caribbean cruise.

"Really?" she asked, as her eyes began to tear up. "Really and truly?"

"Really," I replied. "And truly."

"Oh, honey! This is cause for celebration!"

She did a little happy dance right there in the kitchen, hopping around like she herself had just been kissed for the first time.

"I know," she said, when she was finished dancing. "Let's call your father at work and tell him."

That night one of the boys from the motel unexpectedly

friended me on Facebook. His name was Pinky Faraday. (I know what you're thinking. You're thinking that a guy named Pinky is probably gay, right? Well, he isn't. Not in the least. Pinky is the star of the intermediate baseball team in town and everything. He is taller than me by like a foot; he has dark hair, blue eyes, and a toothy grin that he only flashes when he really means it.) When I called Katie to tell her what had happened, she told me that she thought Pinky was stuck-up and kind of moody. I told her that I thought he was deep and had a lot on his mind. As my Dad would say, we agreed to disagree.

Being Facebook friends with Pinky meant so much to me. It was a big deal and an even bigger surprise because, really, I hadn't done anything to make it happen—it had just happened. And once it happened I felt that it was the next best thing to being popular myself. But to be honest, I wasn't exactly sure why Pinky wanted to be my friend, so I invited him to meet me after school at the Coffee Connection to discuss the matter in person. Naturally, I didn't mention that we were going to discuss our friendship; I just mentioned coffee and maybe tea as options.

Pinky couldn't stay long. He said that his father was giving him and his brothers a hard time lately due to the fact that they had almost burned down the house. He said it wasn't their fault, and I believed him. But still, his father was making them do yard work after school for like a month as a kind of community service.

"How big is your yard?" I asked him, thinking that a month was a long time.

"Not big enough," was his reply.

According to Pinky, his home life wasn't exactly stable. Ever since his father remarried, the Faraday household had been in turmoil because his stepmother had very particular ideas about how they ought to be living, ideas that were far from the way they had been living for as long as anyone could remember. For example, the new Mrs. Faraday was insisting that they all sit down to dinner every night as a family. Pinky was against this sort of thing because they were not, in his opinion, a family. Just because his father had fallen in love with someone did not give that someone the right to decide the eating habits of people she hardly knew. He said that his own mother, when she was alive, allowed everyone in the family to eat when and where they wanted, and as a result holidays were always super special.

"You could count on Christmas and Thanksgiving," Pinky said as he wistfully recalled the past. "We always got together and sometimes nobody left the table for hours. Once my Dad even fell asleep right there at the dining room table and we had to wake him up the next morning for breakfast."

Pinky showed me a picture of his mother that he carried in his wallet. She was a pretty woman with dyed blond hair, blue eyes, and the same bright smile that Pinky had; in fact, her resemblance to Pinky was remarkable. When I pointed it out to him, I noticed that there were tears in his eyes. He told me that he kept a framed copy of the picture next to his bed as well to remind him where he came from.

Pinky was the coolest guy I had ever met because, though he was tough on the outside, he had real feelings and he was not afraid to show them in public. I gave him back the photograph, and we then made a date to see one another again the following week.

FIVE

The Drama Club announced auditions for the winter production of Cole Porter's *Anything Goes*. This is a musical extravaganza featuring plenty of madcap antics aboard an ocean liner bound from New York to London. The score includes such hit songs as "Anything Goes," "You're the Top," and "I Get a Kick Out of You." Of course these were hit songs back in the twentieth century before there was radio, and as a result teenagers today are not as familiar with the work of Cole Porter as they are with, say, Lady Gaga. When I asked Pinky, for instance, if perhaps he and a few of the guys might be interested in trying out for the chorus of *Anything Goes*, he responded by saying, "What's that?" After explaining the plot as well as the process of auditioning for musical theater, everyone including Pinky said that they weren't too interested.

"Sounds gay," said one of the guys.

And that, I thought, was that.

But then the following day, word got around that Tanya Handley had snagged the lead part of Reno Sweeney, an evangelist turned nightclub singer. Tanya put out an unofficial challenge, saying that if any "real men" showed up to audition for the part opposite her, she would personally kiss them on the lips. Pinky and a few of the guys took up the challenge and, though none of them were talented enough to play either the part of Lord Evelyn Oakleigh or Public Enemy #13 Moonface Martin, all of them did get an opportunity to make out with Tanya in the stairwell. Later, when the cast list was posted in the band room, I was super excited (but not surprised) to get the part of Lord Oakleigh. But my thrill was soon multiplied when I learned that Pinky and the guys had all been cast in the chorus.

"Personally," Katie remarked, "I think it's just the idea of being close to Tanya that's getting those guys all worked up."

I told Katie that that was totally understandable due to the fact that Tanya had star quality, and the responsibility of a star is to make everyone feel more excited about everything when she is around. In other words, Tanya was just doing her job, and also Katie was jealous that she hadn't been cast in a lead part.

Since I had been responsible for getting Pinky and his gang to (a) show up and (b) audition, both Katie and Tanya considered me the go-to-guy, and they invited me to take the helm and direct the entire production. My reaction was so over-the-top that Ms. Potter, the teaching supervisor of the Drama Club, had to take several steps back to avoid injury. Once I was finished reacting to the news, I assured everyone present that not only would I consider the job, I would take it and run with it! They would not be disappointed. As I walked away, I remember thinking: life just doesn't get any better than this.

After a week of play practice, I began to realize that this was a bigger challenge than I had thought. Though each day the guys got better and better, they couldn't seem to learn the dance steps that I'd been teaching them, and they had yet to sing a single lyric. It seemed that they could only concentrate on their movements if they were completely silent and stared at their feet, and even then the choreography was a train wreck every time. Nevertheless, I was determined that by opening night they would be good!

One evening after play practice, Pinky and I were walking home together and I explained once again the concept of musical theater by demonstrating the dance steps while singing the lyrics. The air was crisp and cold, and the sky was like a deep blue dream of heaven. I think for the first time in my life I was totally and truly happy. The two of us just ambled along the sidewalks, occasionally stopping to review a dance move or talk about our future. Pinky said that he

was thinking of quitting the show because he didn't consider himself musical comedy material and also rehearsals were interfering with his basketball practice. I told him that one of the first things we learned in the theater as young thespians was that the show must go on. It must.

"How come?" he asked me.

"I don't know," I told him. "It just has to."

The minute I said this, I knew that my mind was made up. My future had been decided, and I had to tell someone.

"Hey," I said to Pinky as we stopped on the pavement. "Can I tell you something that I have never ever told another living soul in my whole life?"

"Sure."

"I have decided that the theater is to be my life."

"Cool," Pinky replied, and he started walking again.

Pinky was so understanding, and all the way home he encouraged me totally in the pursuit of my dream. Even though he didn't have a lick of experience in the field of entertainment, he told me that he could recognize talent when he saw it and, as far as he was concerned, I definitely had whatever was necessary to become a big success. Then he added that anyone with half a brain could see that someone with my kind of passion was going to go very far in this world.

Pinky made it home in time for dinner. But before he went inside the house, he told me that I was special and he wondered why he never noticed me before. He was standing under a streetlight, looking like a superhero. As I walked away, I thought to myself, if someone came to town with a machine gun and threatened to kill Pinky, I'd offer myself instead. He definitely deserved to live.

Zac finally called. I thanked him for getting back to me, but I explained that I couldn't possibly come over. When he asked me why not, I explained how busy I was with rehearsals and all. Also, now that Pinky Faraday and I were BFFs, my schedule wasn't as open as it was when I was in, say, fourth grade. When I wasn't rehearsing, I sometimes went down to watch Pinky shoot hoops, and occasionally Pinky and I met for a hot drink at the Coffee Connection.

Zac told me that I ought to be careful.

"Careful?" I said. "Of what?"

"Of becoming a gay," he answered. "Boys doing it with boys is totally gross, and you can end up a pervert. Or worse."

"Zac?" I said into the phone. "Are you jealous?"

"Don't be a dickhead, dickhead" he said, snarkily. "I'm just saying that up until like yesterday that Pinky kid was totally ignoring you. Now you're like best friends? I just don't like it, that's all."

Zac has always been a big complainer. His specialty is complaining about how people are always treating us as though we're invisible. Some of his favorite comments are:

1) *They didn't even say hello!*

2) *That girl looked right through me!*

3) *Are they just going to pretend we don't exist? HEL-LO?*

Whenever Zac gets like this I explain to him that rather than waiting around for others to say hello or notice him, he'd be much better off DOING something in order to distinguish himself. "You need to make people take notice of you," I tell him. "You need to stand up in order to stand out."

"Right," he said with plenty of sulk in his voice.

"I know!" I offered. "Why don't you get involved in the chorus of *Anything Goes?*"

"You mean like singing and dancing?" he asked.

"It's not too late."

"Dude," he said, deepening his voice. "That is so gay."

SIX

The show went on without a hitch. Tanya was brilliant and her rendition of "Anything Goes" got a standing ovation at both performances. Jed Steckler came down with a wicked case of flu and as a result the audiences never got to enjoy his hilarious portrayal of Public Enemy #13 Moonface Martin. Instead I had to step in at the last moment and double as both Moonface and Lord Oakleigh. It was exhausting—and terrifying. But people came up to me afterwards to tell me that they were utterly amazed, not only because I could play both parts so adroitly and make all of the quick changes, but also because in scenes where both characters appeared, I was able to slip seamlessly between the two without losing my place or my footing. A tour de force, they called it. I was pretty proud.

It turned out to be a good thing that Pinky had dropped out of the show. If he had remained in the chorus, he would have been changing his costume backstage while I did my shtick onstage, and he never would have had the chance to see my performance from out in the auditorium. Besides, after two weeks of rehearsal it didn't seem as though he was ever going to get the dance steps down and do them in a convincing or artistically pleasing manner. I looked for him afterwards, but I totally understood why he didn't hang around. He had said on more than one occasion that he had already endured plenty of the cast's barbed musical-comedy comments and self-congratulatory looks. Everyone was pissed at him for dropping out at the last minute, everyone except for Tanya and me. However, he did call me at home after our cast party to tell me what he thought of the show.

"You are the real star, man."

"But what about Tanya?" I asked him as I was removing my makeup.

"Screw Tanya," he replied bitterly. "She's a stuck-up bitch who thinks too much of herself for her own good."

I couldn't believe my ears; I was so touched. He really thought I was better than Tanya!

He went on to tell me that the situation at home was not good. Apparently his father had been on a rampage for the past twenty-four hours; he had turned the Faraday household upside down—literally. I didn't want to pry, but I did ask him if he was safe. He told me that he was for the time being because he was calling me from the crawl-space up in the attic and that was why he had to whisper.

"If anything happened to you, Pinky," I said, trying to hold back my tears, "I wouldn't be able to go on. I really wouldn't."

"Yes, you would," he said. "You'd be surprised how quickly people get over even the worst stuff."

A chill went up my spine because at that moment I realized that I was going to have to prove to Pinky that he was a person worth not getting over quickly.

"No," I told him. "I wouldn't."

And then very quietly, so that his father wouldn't hear him, we sang a few bars of the song "Anything Goes" together.

The world has gone mad today
And good's bad today,
And black's white today,
And day's night today,
When most guys today
That women prize today
Are just silly gigolos
And though I'm not a great romancer
I know that I'm bound to answer
When you propose,
Anything goes.

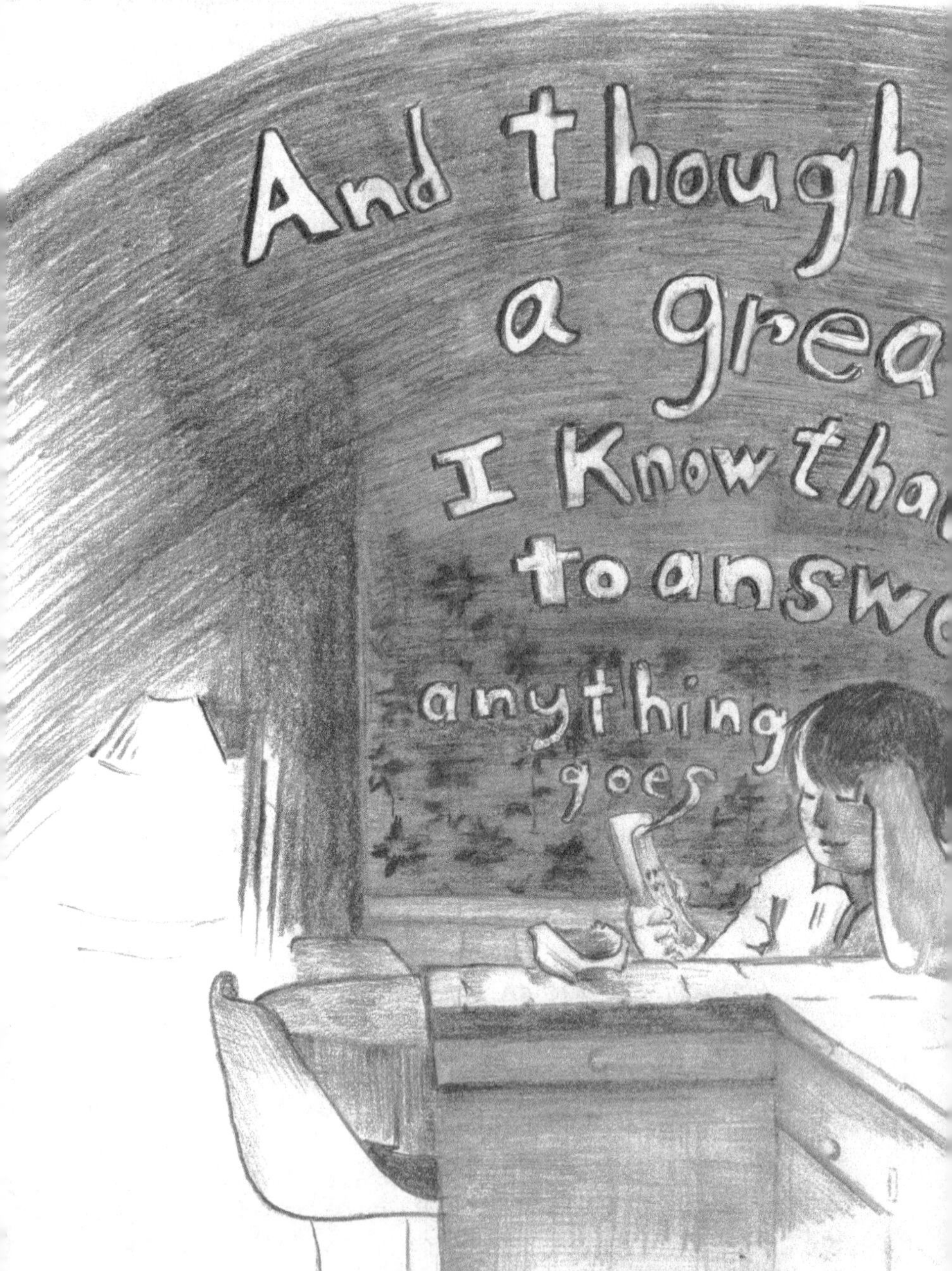
And though
a grea
I Know tha
to answ
anything
goes

I'm not
romancer
I'm bound
when you propose

The next night, I called Pinky on his cell to make sure he was okay and that his father hadn't done anything crazy. When I got no response I texted him several times, sent him a message on Facebook, and then finally called his home phone. His stepmother answered. She was super polite with me, but firm. She said Pinky couldn't speak to me, and I should not try contacting him anymore. I was so stunned I didn't even ask her why. I just said "Okay" and then I hung up.

I sat down and wrote Pinky a long letter telling him what had happened, because I knew he knew nothing about it and was probably being held hostage by his father or something. I hardly slept all night.

The next day at school, I gave Pinky the letter. He took it from me without saying anything and then acted as though he was late for class, which he was not because the bell hadn't even rung yet.

At lunch, he gave me a letter back; it was written on lined paper that had been torn from a spiral notebook and though the writing was nearly illegible, I could make out every word. It said that I was a fairy, a weak person and maybe didn't even deserve to live.

This was devastating news. The worst part of it was that I felt so utterly alone. There was no one in whom I could confide. Katie and Zac had always been jealous of my friendship with Pinky, and they probably would celebrate the fact

that Pinky was finally out of the picture. Dad was away on business, and besides, he wouldn't have understood the problem. And Mom? She would have told me that maybe Pinky wasn't as good a friend as I had thought he was and then suggested that I put the whole thing behind me, call up Zac, and invite him for a sleepover like old times. How could I have told her what was really in my heart? What could she have said if I told her that I didn't want old times or that I wanted Pinky? What nobody could understand, what I could hardly understand myself, was that the one person I wanted to talk to about all this was Pinky. And that just wasn't going to happen. I couldn't exactly walk up to him at school and ask him the one thing I was dying to know—did this mean that he and I were not best friends anymore? Is that what he was trying to tell me? What had I done wrong?

SEVEN

I broke down and told Katie Quinn what happened between Pinky and me, which is to say that I told her that I didn't know what happened between Pinky and me or why he had stopped talking to me. She mentioned that she overheard some of his friends talking about me behind my back.

"What'd they say?" I asked her.

"I shouldn't say,"

"Tell me," I pleaded. "I should know."

"You don't want to know."

"Katie, please. Whatever they said can't be worse than what I'm imagining in my head right now."

"Okay. So the guys were saying you walk like a girl."

Let me just say that this was so much worse than anything that I could have ever imagined in my head. In fact, I felt as though I could have killed myself over this. Naturally, I denied it. I told Katie that I did not walk anything like a girl. I did not! She gave me a sad smile, and then I heard myself saying, "Wait. Do *you* think I walk like a girl?"

"No," was her response, "of course not."

I suggested that the best way to prove that we were both right was to give her a demonstration. Bad move. When I was finished, I turned around and I could tell by the look on her face that something was wrong.

"What?" I asked her.

"Nothing."

I went straight home and threw out my black leotard and sequined cape and all of my glitter makeup. No way was I ever going to dress up as Lady Gaga ever again. That phase of my life was over.

After that I decided to spend some time doing push-ups and also sitting in front of the mirror in my room taking a good hard look at myself. Something was wrong with me and it was definitely showing. But what? No matter how long I stood there in front of the mirror, no matter how hard I stared at my own reflection, I couldn't see the thing that was making me seem different from everybody else. My life had become an obvious tragedy; ironic that I was the only person who couldn't see it.

The next day at school Pinky stopped saying *hey* to me in between classes, and he seemed to be going out of his way to avoid me in the cafeteria. English class was a particular kind of torture because I was forced to see him for forty minutes, and he refused to look at me or acknowledge my existence. No one knew how deeply I suffered over this because I was determined to keep it to myself. This went on for more than a week, and the whole time I just wanted to know what had happened to my friendship with Pinky. Where did it go? What had I done to upset him? Was it because I walked like a girl? Maybe there was something I could do to make it better. But what?

Then Mr. Kienast asked me to read aloud from my report on the short story. This was like a form of torture specially designed to humiliate and embarrass me. As I made my way to the front of the class, I could hear the kids whispering behind my back. *That's the kid who has a crush on Pinky Faraday.* This was the longest walk I had ever taken in my life. I stood there facing the class with my stupid paper, and even though I knew it wasn't possible, I hoped that maybe this was all just a bad dream. When I realized that it wasn't a bad dream, I hoped instead that I might drop dead in front of the entire class. When that didn't happen, I swallowed hard and began.

"I chose for my topic *The Loss of Innocence as Reflected in Literature.* Here's what I wrote:

> "The loss of innocence is brought about because of an experience with no explanation. The character must be involved in the experience

and must experience the loss. Must be hurt. Must survive. The experience must be potent enough to be remembered and must create a subtle change in the character . . ."

Mr. Kienast gave me an A for my report. No one could tell that I copied it all from a book. Pinky continued to ignore me, and for the rest of the day I was officially invisible.

EIGHT

Mom was cleaning my room, and she just *happened* to read something that I'd been typing on my computer, a confidential email that I could have sent to my BFF—if I'd had a BFF. But since I do not have a BFF, or even a close friend in whom I could confide my deepest and most intimate feelings, the email was just idling on my screen unread—until Mom came along.

She had a fit and then we had an all-out fight. I told her that my private life was none of her business and maybe I was crazy but it seemed to me that I ought to be able to have the freedom to express my own private thoughts in the privacy of my own room and on my own "personal" computer. She claimed that I was still too young to have any kind of a life that didn't concern her, personal, private, or otherwise.

"I'm your mother," she said louder than was absolutely

necessary. "And in case you haven't noticed, I am in charge of your life."

To express my opposition to this extremely unfair point of view and to protest against people feeling that they had the right to read emails without the say-so of the person who wrote them, I attempted to run away to San Francisco. I did not leave a note. I simply packed a bag and snuck out through the garage. Unfortunately, I only got as far as the bus station. Mom dragged me back home so that she could tell me that she was very, very, very worried about me (she used three *very*'s). She sat me down in the living room and announced that we needed to have a talk.

"A talk?" I said.

"Yes," she replied. "For example, do you think you might be depressed?"

"Um," I remarked. "I'm not sure. I don't think so."

She then went on to explain that depression can often go undetected, but if left untreated it could become a serious problem in the life of a teen. Apparently, drug abuse and self-loathing are possible next steps when depression is involved—and worse.

"Worse?"

She didn't care to elaborate. Instead she told me that she couldn't even begin to imagine what it must be like for me to be a teenager living in the modern world. When she was my age, the world was an entirely different place and there were no such things as the Internet or Facebook or cell phones or texting or tweeting, and computers hadn't even been invented yet.

"But how did you communicate with your friends?" I asked her.

"By speaking to them," she replied. "Either face-to-face or on the telephone."

She explained that when she was growing up, they only had one telephone and it was located in the hallway of the house. Her sisters, her mother and father, everyone knew all about her business. And though at the time she resented the fact that she was not allowed to have secrets, she had come to realize that her family was able to help her simply because they always knew what she was going through.

"So that's why I was wondering," Mom said. "Are you going through something I should know about?"

When I didn't respond, she pulled out my art history notebook, opened it, and showed me the inside cover. There, alongside a pencil sketch of some random fruits and an earthenware jug, Pinky's name was doodled in script. Each letter was carefully shaded and colored. Then she slowly turned the pages, showing me other examples of Pinky's name written over and over in all the margins.

"That's Katie's notebook," I blurted out. "She loaned it to me. It's not mine, if that's what you're thinking."

Mom's shoulders dropped and she let out a sigh of either

defeat or relief. As she stood up, she handed me the note-book and said: "Well, let's make sure that Katie gets it back."

And then to signal that our talk was over, she leaned over and took me in her arms. She hugged me hard for like a full minute until I said, "Mom? I kind of can't breathe." I don't think she knew that I was lying to her about the notebook, but I'm pretty sure she knew I wasn't telling the truth.

After that, I was bigger than TV in our house, and that's saying a lot. Mom kept a close eye on me, and Dad was pretty interested in my moods and whereabouts as well. I was like the star of my own reality series, except for the fact that the only people watching were my mother and father. And I wasn't on just once a week; I was broadcasting every day, all day.

Dad came into my room one evening, sat on my bed, and asked if there was maybe something I wanted to discuss with him. I watched as little beads of sweat began to form on his brow. His leg twitched and though he tried to hold my gaze, his eyes kept shifting toward the door as though he was sizing up the exits in case of an emergency. I knew that Mom had put him up to this and I could tell that he wanted to go back downstairs and watch his show on TV. I took pity on him and said, "I'm good." He gave me a pat on the shoulder and told me that any time I needed to talk with him, mano-a-mano, he was available 24-7.

NINE

Meanwhile school continued to be dreaded and horrible. Whose idea was school anyway? A sadist's, no doubt. For example, my particular form of torture was being trapped in an environment in which everyone was going around saying that I was gay. Whether I am gay or not is not the issue. The issue is this: it is wrong to declare someone *else*'s sexuality, and it is equally wrong to go around demanding that someone declare his or her own sexuality if he or she doesn't feel like it. Just because you yourself happen to be uncomfortable with uncertainty and can't stand ambiguity and/or paradox, does not mean that everyone in the world is wired in the same way. Some of us prefer to remain a mystery—even to ourselves—until we are ready.

The GSA-ers were the worst; they claimed that I was in denial, and they told me to my face (repeatedly) that if I would just admit my homosexual tendencies I would feel a whole lot better about myself. I thought they were just trying to up their membership and make it seem as though the Gay-Straight-Alliance was a real club with actual members instead of a fringe group of geeks with dyed hair and pierced eyebrows. I told them (repeatedly) that I would feel a whole lot better if they would just leave me alone, which of course they didn't seem to want to do. They suggested that I consider labeling myself "Questioning" and leave it at that. Or maybe I could declare myself an "ally." I asked them why I needed a label at all; why did I need to declare myself as anything other than Trevor? Isn't that enough?

Miranda Lemley, a sophomore with a round face, sparkly blue eyes, baggy pants, perfunctory piercings, and an impressive grill of dental work, sighed hard. As she fussed with her green Mohawk, she said, "Look, Travis, we're just trying to be friendly. You seem lost and lonely. Once upon a time we were the same way, so we thought you could use a kind word. But if you're gonna be that way about it, forget we ever said anything." She then turned on her heel and walked away. The others followed after her.

"TREVOR," I called out after her. "My name is Trevor!"

The jocks also began to taunt and abuse me. Without Pinky and his posse around to provide a little street cred, I might as well have been wearing a target on my back. In addition to *Faggot*, some of the names they called me to my face were as follows: *Fruit Loop*, *Poof*, *Sissy*, *Girlyboy*, *Nellie*,

Big Nell-box, Nancy, Mary, and *Evelyn.* There was a large football player named Turk who apparently decided that his mission in life was to make my life extra miserable. Why Turk felt the need to pick on *me* when there happened to be so many other kids in our school who were weaker, more defenseless, and (excuse me for saying it) more deserving, remains a mystery to this day. In any case, Turk found it in his heart to jab me with his fist, his elbow, his knee, his thumb, a book, or whatever he had handy whenever I passed him in the hallway. And because he was the king of the jocks, his minions did the same. As a way of defending myself I tried to make myself invisible, but again and again I was unable to activate that particular superpower. At night, I busied myself by deleting the hateful comments that were posted to my Facebook wall. It was exhausting work, but the thought that Pinky might be checking out my profile and could possibly see these remarks made me work even harder and I was kept up late into the night.

Sometimes to entertain myself I tried to imagine the unhappy futures that were in store for my fellow schoolmates. For example, I envisioned Turk living in a one-bedroom, low-rise apartment with a partial view of an unremarkable third-tier American city. I imagined that by the age of 30 Turk would be stuck in a job that went nowhere and meant nothing. He would have neither a wife nor a girlfriend, maybe a cat. His football trophies would be placed prominently on top of his TV, but only he would admire them. Most nights he would sit there trying to figure out where he went wrong. How did it happen that one day he was so on top of the world and then practically overnight he was nothing, no one? Then one evening after months and months of soul-searching, it would come to him in a flash. *I see now,* he would say to himself. *I should've been nicer to that Trevor kid back in high school. Everything in my life would be different if I just hadn't been so outright mean to him.* Later that evening he would get the idea to call me so he could make it up to me personally, tell me that he was sorry before it was too late. He would look me up on Facebook, and when he couldn't find me there he'd go to the White Pages website and do a search. Sadly, he would not be able to find me there either because it would be too late. I'd already be dead.

TEN

I came home from my piano lesson and found Father Joe sitting on our living room sofa. He looked like a dark cloud in his priestly blacks and clerical collar, but a cloud with a big smile and a firm handshake. Right away, he offered to take me to the Dairy Queen. I was suspicious from the start. First of all, we were never that religious as a family. Yes, we believed in God, but we were never that big on His local representatives regardless of their affiliation. For example, I can't remember any one of them being invited into our house. Ever. Father Joe and I drove across town to the Dairy Queen in Father Joe's blue, midsize Malibu, and the whole time he asked me questions about my schoolwork, about how I was getting on with Mom and Dad, and about the kids at school.

Father Joe had a big doughy face with features that were unremarkable: nose, lips, eyes, and chin were all standard issue, not one of them stood out among the others. I noticed that his hands were unnaturally clean and he kept his fingernails neatly clipped. Dandruff dotted his shoulders like the first bit of snow on a paved street. And the whole time he was talking, I couldn't help wondering if he had ever kissed a girl. Did he turn against a life of sex and then decide to devote himself to God, or was it the other way around? Did he find God and then force himself to forgo the sex altogether? Either way, it seemed a shame. Not that I was interested in having sex with Father Joe. Please. But still, shouldn't everyone have the right to enjoy themselves in this world? Shouldn't everyone be loved? And why would God want a person to *not* have sex? What would be the point of that?

Anyway, he parked the Malibu around the side of the building, and as he ran down the list of ice cream treats we might enjoy, I found myself actually praying: *Please, God, do not let anyone from school see me in the company of a priest on a Saturday afternoon. No offense, but it will ruin me.*

Instead of accompanying Father Joe into the place, I opted to stay in the car and wait for him to bring me a hot-fudge sundae. And it's a good thing because, as I was going through the glove compartment (a Bible, a pack of tissues, a county map, a bottle of aspirin, the registration, and a book of matches from a bar called The Hideaway), I happened to look up and spot Miranda Lemley walking into the Dairy Queen with a few of her lesbian friends. I thanked God for saving me the embarrassment of being recognized, and promised to do charitable works for the rest of my life. Eventually, Father Joe returned to the car and, just as I was about to dig into my sundae, he introduced the topic of sex.

"What about it?" I inquired.

Father Joe seemed to be under the impression that I didn't know where babies came from or how they got made. Before I could correct this misperception, he launched into a description of the process, giving me a blow-by-blow account of what men and women get up to when they are naked with each other. It was only then that I began to realize this whole outing had been a miserable set-up between my parents and Father Joe.

"So then the man's penis becomes blood engorged," said Father Joe as he reached for his soft drink and took a sip. "He gets hard."

How was it possible that this was happening? Why hadn't I seen it coming? I felt like a total stooge.

"And then the man inserts his penis into the vagina of the woman, which is lubricated in its own natural juices."

I swear it was like gag city.

And then just when I was grossed out to the max and humiliated to the point of never wanting to have sex with a single living person for the rest of my totally sorry life, Father Joe turned to me and said: "Trevor, have you ever had desires? And I'm talking about sexual desires for another boy."

I decided that in fact this was not happening; it was a bad dream. It was a nightmare and I'd be waking up in my bed in just a moment. Wake up, I told to myself. Wake up! Wake up! I tried to scream, but I found that just like in a dream, I couldn't. WAKE UP!

"Be honest with me, Trevor. I can help you if you are honest."

I looked away, hoping that by removing Father Joe from my sight I might somehow make him disappear from the

face of the earth or at least from my vicinity; it didn't work. I was still trapped in a nightmare, and he kept talking, making it worse.

"Have you, for example, ever wanted to touch another boy . . . like . . . and I'm not suggesting anything here, but, like Pinky Faraday?"

After that I can't remember much of what was said. I completely blocked him out, and all of my powers of concentration were focused on devising a getaway plan. I briefly considered opening the car door, leaping from my seat, and throwing myself into the oncoming highway traffic, but every time I took hold of the door handle, something made me pause. Eventually, Father Joe stopped talking, drove me back home, and dropped me off, but not without first promising that we would do this again real soon. What I wanted to say was: *Just kill me now.*

"How was your visit with Father Joe?" Mom called out from the kitchen.

"Fine," I replied as I ran up the stairs and into my room.

After what they'd put me through, I felt entirely justified in not mentioning my plans. Mom and Dad did not need to know that the following day I was going to start a new life. That was my business. But just so that the plan would remain fresh in my mind, I sat down at my desk and wrote it all out longhand.

MY PLAN

Dye hair and eye lashes.

Change name, identity.

Change schools.

MapQuest Mexico.

Change religion.

ELEVEN

They say that when you die your whole life flashes before you, but what they don't tell you is that the very last day is the worst day of all and you'd rather not replay it. There are no statistics, but I'm guessing that the last day is the final straw, proof that your life was so not worth living.

The toilet in the master bathroom flushed—a sure sign in our house that the day had officially begun. Mom was up. I could hear her humming.

Mister T, our cat, was downstairs, wide awake and waiting to be released into the wilds of the backyard in order to begin his daily business of disturbing (and possibly killing) whatever wildlife he can sink his teeth into. Mister T is a real terrorist, but rather than targeting a particular population such as field mice or house wrens, he likes to spread his enmity all around to include everything and everyone in view. We humans are especially subject to his disapproval. Only my mother seems to be exempt from being clawed, chased, hissed at, scratched, and bitten on a regular basis. I suspect that Mister T considers Mom necessary for his survival. When it comes to the rest of us, he either hisses at us in order to get us to understand that we are sitting in his spot or takes a swipe to let us know who is boss.

I've read stories on the Internet about how cats are supposed to know when a person is close to death. Apparently household cats have extrasensory powers that tell them to sleep outside the door of the soon-to-be-deceased. Possible? Sure. But no one has been able to prove it. Personally, I think it's just an urban legend, the result of that weird aura cats give off like swamp gas. In any case, Mister T would not be the right cat to study in order to prove this premise, because on any given day of the week, he could care less whether I am dead or alive. Most mornings he just sits at the back door, occasionally licking his chops, cleaning his paws, and waiting for my mother to open the back door and let him loose upon another unsuspecting day. Like everybody else in the house, Mister T had no idea what I was planning for myself.

I figured that if I actually went through with my plan, I would be spared the torture of having to face another day (i.e., Turk and the kids in the cafeteria). I was counting on this whole charade being over and done with and hoping that some kind of eternal silence would descend like snow falling on Christmas morning. In other words, I was looking forward to being done with this world.

But . . .

What if death wasn't really the end of everything? I mean no one really knows for sure what happens after you die. I've read about the afterlife on the Internet. People who died and then came back to life always say how peaceful their dead bodies appeared to be while they themselves were floating up near the ceiling looking down on the whole deathbed scene. I was looking forward to that kind of peace. In fact, I couldn't wait. I imagined the dead quiet, the eternal peace, the ceiling, the floating, the end.

But what if I was forced to witness the whole unhappy course of events that followed on the heels of my death? Suppose I had to stand by and watch my mother discover my dead body lying on the bed? That would be awful, and I wasn't sure that I could handle it.

Imagine that I'm sprawled out on the bed, staring up at the ceiling, eyes wide open, but seeing nothing. This time instead of just pretending that I'm dead, like I used to do on occasion, I am actually and truly dead. Mom walks into the room, sees me lying there, and freezes.

When she realizes what's going on, she lets out an involuntary scream. But in order not to wake Dad, she quickly catches herself and covers her mouth with both hands. She shuts the door. All the color has drained from my face and my skin has a bluish tint, making me look more than a little ghoulish. The color has drained from Mom's face too, but she is still alive. She falls down onto the carpet and, while kneeling beside the bed, she takes hold of my shoulders, shakes me, and repeats the words, "Why, why, why?" over and over. My face is cold as stone but I look relaxed, peaceful, and almost happy. My plaid Converse high-tops are lying on the floor beside the bed, their mouths wide open and tongues hanging out. Mom picks up one of the sneakers, looks at it as if it is something that's fallen from outer space, and then she unexpectedly presses it to her heart. I am forced to watch her as she starts to sob uncontrollably. I don't say anything. I can't. I'm up near the ceiling, dead. And besides, what would I say? "It's going to be all right. Don't worry, Mom, I'll do better next time." No. I just have to float there and endure her heartache until the pain becomes too much and I am forced to fly off to God knows where.

This was the kind of thinking that could sometimes discourage me from going through with my plan. But then I would tell myself, "*It's a good thing that your mind is made up. Now all you need are the means to do it.*"

TWELVE

Most mornings while waiting for the school bus, I sit on the front stoop of our house and daydream. Because my present is usually too horrible to think about, I spend a lot of the time imagining various futures for myself, all of them fantastic and amazing.

I was someone leading an extreme and glamorous life somewhere in the tropics.

I was famous and everyone wanted to be photographed in my presence.

I had a three-picture deal with a major movie studio.

Lady Gaga and I were best friends; we were a team, touring the world together. I designed her outfits and pyrotechnical displays; she bought me a car.

The thought of these various career opportunities kept me very busy in my mind; they passed the time. But that spring, as my popularity diminished to the point that even I didn't

want to hang out with myself, I realized Mexico wasn't going to cut it and I began to imagine what it would be like if I died an early death.

I practiced for my funeral. For long stretches I would lie on my bed in my best and only suit. I lit candles and incense. I looked great, peaceful. And I imagined people coming up to my coffin, one by one and paying their last respects. Many of them cried. People I hardly knew said things like: *I should've seen it coming. We had no idea. I could've been nicer to him. Who knew that he was suffering? He was always such a cheerful child.* Anyway, the funeral thing just made me feel better about the whole situation, and I began to consider it as a real option.

I began to delete certain pictures of myself from my phone and from my computer. I wanted only the ones that I considered flattering to remain after I was gone. I organized my poems and made a file of the ones that I especially liked, the ones that best expressed my life journey. My play, *Nevermore the Wind*, which had been announced as part of the Spring Dramathon, was printed, copied, and bound. The dedication read: To anyone who has ever heard the wind.

I deleted the movie of Pinky that I had on my camera. It wasn't a secret. At the time, I told him I was recording it so that we could review it later and work on his dance steps, but he had already quit the show by the time I had it fully edited. In the movie, he looked so handsome, slightly sweaty, and totally into the task at hand. Sometimes as a form of personal torture I would sit in my room and view it over and over. Even though his dancing sucked and he had no stage presence, he was a bright beacon of hope up on that stage; he knew how to laugh at himself and that made people smile. To me, he represented all kinds of possibilities that I could not have articulated at the time. Still can't.

When you're young, people tell you that you'll get over stuff; they say it as though what you're feeling isn't really real or it's just practice for what comes later on in life. But what we have now is all that matters. The love we feel today is what we know of love; good or bad, it's what we've got to work with. People don't recognize that sometimes a feeling is so intense it makes you just want to lay down and die rather than go on feeling it. I'm not saying that that's a good thing; I'm just saying that it happens. And I know because it happened to me.

Anyway, I missed the bus that morning. I guess I was concentrating so hard on the future that I missed what was happening right then and there. Both Zac and Katie saw me running after the bus, but rather than make the driver stop for me, they just laughed at me as they drove off.

I was late for school and had to go to the office. Usually Mrs. Rodriguez gives you a note and then she makes some kind of mark under your name in The Book of Lateness. Also all first-period teachers have perfected a scowl suitable for latecomers, but that's about all that happens. No big deal. Life goes on. But that day, Mrs. Rodriguez came out from behind her barricade and told me that Principal Davis wanted to see me right away in her office.

"I'm so sorry about all this, Trevor," Principal Davis said as soon as she hung up the phone. "I really am. And we are doing everything we can to get to the bottom of it and find out who is responsible."

I felt a little crazy because I had no idea what she was talking about, and the more she kept on assuring me that everything was going to be all right, the more I was starting to freak. I felt like I was in that Franz Kafka short story, the one we read in English class about the guy who wakes up and discovers he's been changed into a bug, but doesn't realize it until it's too late.

"Do *you* know anything about how this might've happened?" she asked me.

I did not. And by that point I was so alarmed by what *it* might turn out to be that I just shook my head and left it at that.

"Would you like to call your parents?"

Again, I shook my head, this time more vigorously.

Mom and Dad have told me again and again that I am not to call them at work unless it is a real emergency. And since I didn't know the nature of the problem, I technically couldn't consider it as such. And what's more, I really didn't want to know.

"I have to go home," I told Principal Davis.

"Of course, of course," she replied, nodding her head and giving me a look of serious concern. "Shall I have someone drive you?"

"No, thanks. The walk will be good for me. The fresh air and all."

My plan was to make a quick stop at my locker, ditch my gym clothes and pick up a few things that I might need just in case I never came back to school. The hallways were deserted and I could almost feel the walls and floors breathing a sigh of relief. In about five minutes the place would be heaving with the jostle of a thousand teenagers, each of whom had very specific fears and hopes and loves and disappointments; it was a volatile mix and I was happy to be relieved of it, even if it was just for one day. I was sure that the cause for Principal Davis's concern would be revealed soon enough, and that I wasn't going to like it. In any case, it could wait.

As I turned the corner, I could see Mr. Hooper at the far end of the hallway, standing by my locker with his back to me. He was wearing his usual janitor uniform: khaki shirt with his name embroidered in script above the pocket, khaki pants with keys dangling from his belt, dust-colored work boots, and a wool hat featuring our school colors and team mascot. As I got closer I could see the collection of paint cans, rags, and brushes that he had lined up on the floor beside him. He was so into his work that he didn't notice my approach. In fact, I stood right beside him for what seemed like about a year. I had plenty of time to read, over and over, the letters that had been deliberately scratched into my locker.

F.

A.

G.

G.

O.

T.

"Oh," said Mr. Hooper, startled by my presence. "This your locker, huh?"

At that moment, the bell rang, doors flew open, and the hall began to fill with the teaming masses. All I knew was that I had to get out of there before anyone saw me. I took off down the hall, my eyes fixed on the emergency exit door and the world beyond.

THIRTEEN

D̶ear Mom and Dad,

I don't want you to think I haven't given this a lot of thought, because I have. I tried to cure myself, but nothing worked. Don't think it's your fault. It's not. It just happens. I'm different and there is nothing in this world that's going to make that change. Please give all my Lady Gaga DVDs and posters to Katie Quinn who happens to love Lady G. as much as I do. And please, if it's possible, play "Born This Way" at my funeral. It says everything. It's the title song from her second album and it's my absolute fave. And don't cry too much. It would've been a skillion times worse if I had lived.

Your loving son,
Trevor

FOURTEEN

FIFTEEN

The people at the hospital informed me that a person cannot commit suicide by taking too many aspirin. But they pretty much guaranteed me that I wouldn't have a headache for like another year.

I think they were kidding.

Mom and Dad were by my bedside when I woke up, and I could tell by the state of their faces that they'd been crying. They kept saying how sorry they were for everything. And even though I kept assuring them that it wasn't their fault, they couldn't take it in. They seemed very determined to make up for it somehow or at least to make it right. It was kind of sweet to watch them in action. Dad canceled all his business trips for the next month. He said that he was going to stay home and teach me to play football.

"Really, Dad," I told him. "Go to work. I hate football. Seriously."

"Well, then, something," he said, looking at me with the saddest set of eyes I've ever seen on a man.

Mom kept blaming herself for missing the cues. She said things like, "I should've known." Or "Why didn't I see it coming?" I tried to comfort her by reminding her that she had a lot on her plate. She told me, "That's no excuse. You're my kid, and I'm going to do better from now on. And we're going to see a therapist. Together. All three of us."

Great. Football and therapy.

Suicide turned out to be not the greatest idea in terms of my future options. I was suddenly looking at a life in which I was trapped, grounded, and suspect. But I guess it was way better than the life of quiet desperation that I'd been quietly and desperately living. We are all in it together now. And of course I am alive.

Zac came walking into my hospital room with eyes downcast and hands clasped together in altar boy fashion. He looked like a guy who was being forced to view the open coffin at his best friend's funeral—not crying, but wanting to. The minute he looked up and saw me lying in the hospital bed, he broke down sobbing into my bed sheet. He said that if I ever tried anything like that again he'd kill me with his bare hands. Then he insisted that I give him the names of every kid in school who was ever mean to me because he was going to totally kick their asses.

Sweet.

Fortunately Katie had gone to visit her aunt and she wasn't expected back until after the weekend. We all agreed that it would be better if she didn't know about "my little episode" (as Mom called it). If Katie found out that she had missed an opportunity to save my life or nurse me back to health, she'd be bitterly disappointed. And also Katie didn't really understand the concept of keeping a secret. I mean she understood that a secret is confidential; it's just that the number of people in whom she had confidence was very large. The news would have spread throughout the school and for the remainder of my high school years I'd be a famous head case—a situation I could definitely do without.

Thankfully, my stay at the hospital was brief. But while I was there I had an opportunity to meet a nurse named Jack. Jack was super nice. Actually, Jack was a candy striper, which is almost like a nurse, only younger. Jack was full of all kinds of interesting information. For example, he told me that he believed people who committed suicide just had to come back and live a whole lifetime all over again.

"Good to know," I told him, as he plumped my pillow. "Because the thought of growing up again with my parents makes me totally depressed. Once around the block with them is plenty."

He laughed and said that it didn't work that way. "You wouldn't necessarily come back into the same family and all."

"Right," I replied. "But knowing my luck, I would."

He gave me some advice, which I didn't mind taking because once upon a time he himself had been through something just like I had. He suggested that I might want to find someone I can talk on a regular basis about my problems.

"Y'mean, like a shrink?" I asked, thinking that maybe he considered me a lunatic.

"Or like a friend," he replied. "Someone you can trust." When he said that, the gravity of the situation hit me. What if I'd actually died? When I thought about how I might have never met Jack, or how sad my parents would've been without me, or how Zac and Katie might have lost a friend forever, I turned my face to the wall and started to cry. Jack didn't seem surprised, he even had a tissue box handy.

"What do I do now?" I asked him between sobs. He lightly touched my shoulder and then quietly reminded me that I didn't have to *do* anything today other than breathe. He said that starting tomorrow I might want to consider living my life one day at a time. No big decisions. Just for a while. Stay in the moment. As much as I can. Appreciate what's right in front of me. I looked at him and told him that I'd give it a try.

He made me promise that I would never do anything like kill myself, and if I ever thought about doing harm to myself I was to call him right away. He scribbled his cell phone number on the back of the tissue box and handed it to me.

"*I promise*," I thought, clutching the box to me. I didn't say it out loud, but maybe it wasn't necessary. Jack looked to me like a friend, someone I would be able to trust someday, someone I might call.

The next day, just as I was leaving the hospital with Mom and Dad, Zac showed up and stopped us in the hallway. His eyes were wild with excitement, the way they get when he discovers a new constellation through the lens of his high-powered telescope, like he's taken in too much light.

Anyway, he wanted to know what I was doing on Saturday. I thought he was going to give me information about some totally deadbeat support group for gay, suicidal teenagers, so I told him that I was all set.

"Oh," he replied.

But then he pulled out what looked like two tickets from his pocket and added: "'Cause yours truly scored two tickets to the Lady Gaga concert Saturday night. I thought, well . . . if it's okay with your parents, it might be fun for you and me to go. Whatd'ya think?"

Mom and Dad looked at one another and then agreed that it was my call as long as I felt up to it. Okay, so maybe it was just the tickets, but right then and there I made a decision—I was going to live.

At least until Saturday.

AFTERWORD

At the start of my sophomore year of high school I was assigned to Mr. Shust's English class. He was a cranky and fastidious man of middle years who dressed in tweeds and flannel and insisted that his students keep a journal. He told us that the experience would enrich our lives (whatever that meant) and we would be graded not on the quality of our writing, but on our willingness to participate. So every evening after my homework was finished, I dutifully made an entry into the black-and-white speckled composition book. I began by chronicling the minor and major moments of my life, the hurts, hopes, and heartbreaks, and after a while writing became a habit. When I entered my twenties, I had a shelf filled with a written record of my adolescent years. These notebooks certainly came in handy years later, when I began the difficult work of becoming a writer.

One morning, while sitting at my desk and sipping coffee, I heard a news report about teen suicide on the radio. According to statistics then, a young person who identified as gay or lesbian was three to four times more likely to attempt suicide than his or her heterosexual peers, and 33% of all teen suicides involved homosexual kids. I was appalled by this fact, and shocked that nothing was being done to prevent the loss of what I considered our greatest natural resource—our youth. Instinctively, I turned to my old journals and I began to read. For the first time in years, I was reminded of just how confusing it was for me as an adolescent—how painful and lonely. There on those pages was my story. I immediately wrote the first few lines of a story about a thirteen-year-old boy who confides to his journal. I called him Trevor.

> Dear Diary,
>   Tonight I walked into the living room while Mom and Dad were watching TV. Fell dead to the floor. No response from them. I think that television reruns have replaced their natural spontaneity. I mean, unless I'm on the eleven o'clock news, I don't think they'd care. And even then they might sleep through it.

Eventually Trevor discovers that he is different—different from his parents, different from his schoolmates, and different from his best friend. *Trevor* is a poignant and humorous portrait of a boy in crisis, but it's also about anyone who has ever felt as though they just can't get it right and they don't fit in no matter how hard they try.

It wasn't that difficult to find the inspiration for Trevor. All of us have felt this way at one time or another, especially during our teenage years when we are just beginning to piece together the story of ourselves. Fortunately, my story was close at hand and my journals were stuffed with poems, rants, dreams, prayers, vows, ideas, and remembrances of what it meant to be fourteen, fifteen, sixteen . . . The irony was that just as I was beginning to discover myself, I was becoming a stranger to the people I loved the most—my family. I felt that they couldn't know me, not *really*, because if they knew who I was they would most certainly reject me. I couldn't live with that—not even as a possibility. And so I kept myself a secret from them, moved further and further away from them, and began to explore life and love without them.

I went on to perform *Trevor* onstage as part of my solo show, *Word of Mouth*, and eventually the show found its way to the HBO Comedy Festival in Aspen and then Off-Broadway where, incredibly, I won the prestigious New York Drama Desk Award for best solo performance of that year. One night following a performance of *Word of Mouth*,

I met Randy Stone and Peggy Rajsk, and they asked me to consider writing the screenplay for a short film based on the story of *Trevor*.

The resulting 18-minute film (produced by Randy Stone and directed and produced by Peggy Rajski) went on to win many awards, including an Academy Award for Best Live Action Short. It was an exciting time as we watched our little film find an audience and spread the word that gay was okay—and during a period when LGBT issues were just beginning to find their way into the news. The times were changing and *Trevor* was in some small way able to contribute to that change. In 1997 when we sold the film to HBO, we thought it might be a good idea to flash a telephone number at the end in case there happened to be a kid out there who could relate to the character of Trevor and needed someone to talk to. We wanted to let young people know that it was all right to reach out and ask for help. Someone would always be standing by to listen to their problems. But after doing some research we found that there was no national 24-hour crisis intervention and suicide prevention lifeline for gay teens. And so we set out to create one.

Three months later, The Trevor Project was launched, and finally lesbian, gay, bisexual, transgender, and questioning teens had a place to turn. That first night we received over 1,500 calls, and we've been at it ever since. Every year we receive approximately 30,000 calls from young people around the country. Of course, not every call requires a rescue and not all of the young people identify as LGBT, but every call comes from someone who is struggling with issues of identity and is a person between the ages of 13 and 24 who is in need of someone who will listen. Thrown out of their homes, shunned by friends, often with no one to whom they can turn, these young people have found the help they need simply by calling 1-800-4-U-Trevor.

These days, young adult novels are full of complex lesbian and gay characters. Twenty-first century authors like David Levithan, Alex Sanchez, Jacqueline Woodson, Bill Konigsberg, and Mayra Lazara Dole write eloquently and often about the issues affecting the lives of LGBT teens. In fact, while perusing recent YA publishing lists of any major house, one might get the idea that it's not such a bad time to be a teen who is LGBT-identified. But amazingly and alarmingly, the statistics today remain no better than they were over twenty years ago when I first sat down to write *Trevor*. LGBT youth are still killing themselves and statistics indicate that they are four times more likely to attempt suicide than their heterosexual peers. Fortunately, The Trevor Project continues to provide every young person with a place they can go to receive the encouragement they need to live fully and with hope, and, most importantly, the support they need to keep on living life.

Recently Dan Savage's very successful "It Gets Better" campaign created a viral revolution and allowed adults to send out a message loud and clear to youth that life would indeed get better, if only they could hang on a bit longer. It also helped The Trevor Project become the go-to organization for youth who are struggling with their sexuality and identity. As a result, our call volume has spiked. We opened a third call center, which is located in Harvey Milk's old camera shop in San Francisco, and which is dedicated to Harvey's memory. We've also taken a much more active role in communicating to youth that we are here for them 24/7. In addition to the lifeline, we've designed outreach and educational programs. We launched TrevorSpace last year, a secure online destination where youth can connect with one another, offer one another peer-to-peer support, and share information, and less than a year later we have close to 20,000 registered and active members. Another feature we have developed is *Ask Trevor*, through which young people can write in and ask questions that are not time sensitive, and read our responses online. We have launched *Trevor Chat*, an online destination where teens can chat with a trained counselor and get some guidance *before* a crisis occurs. We have also been instrumental in introducing anti-bullying legislation on the state and federal level. We even have an in-school program where we train educators and students, meeting youth, on their home turf and talking to them about the power of words and the value of listening.

Despite all these new developments and online services, we remain first and foremost a lifeline, offering voice-to-voice communication, saving lives, and working to normalize help-seeking behavior. In a world that is becoming increasingly depersonalized because of digital media, we remain dedicated to providing every young person, regardless of his or her identity, the opportunity to be heard—and they needn't wait until a crisis occurs to call on us. If I had understood at fourteen that asking for help is an essential part of the human experience, I might have been able to get the help I needed sooner rather than later.

Of course, there is still much to do for youth everywhere. The passing of the Marriage Equality Act in New York State was a great win for youth who believe in the power of love, but the love of a teen in Texas is not yet equal to one living in New York, Connecticut, Iowa, Massachusetts, New Hampshire, Vermont, or Washington, DC. And further afield, homosexuality is illegal in more than 30 African nations, and in some places is a crime punishable by death. In some Islamic countries like Iran, Saudi Arabia, Sudan, and Yemen, homosexuals face imprisonment, corporal punishment, or in some cases, execution. The globe has shrunk to the size of the worldwide web and every young person has access it. They get the message, they hear the news, and we are working hard to incorporate their experiences into the stories they see and hear. Martin Luther King, Jr. once said: "A threat to justice anywhere is a threat to justice everywhere," and his wisdom has perhaps never been better applied than to the struggle to make one person's love equal to everybody else's—regardless of gender, race, or sexual orientation.

Changing the story of LGBT and Questioning youth throughout the world and giving them the right to love is one way to ensure a better and more loving future for everyone. Young people, all of them, belong to our future, and without them we cannot realize tomorrow. Convincing even one kid that his or her life is worth living is to convince ourselves that the world itself is worth saving. I believe that all young people need to find stories they can believe in, stories that will bring them closer to understanding that they are perfect exactly as they are. I hope Trevor's story can be just that for generations to come.

Enjoy!

James
September 2011

ACKNOWLEDGMENTS

I t would be easy to say that the story of *Trevor* has had a life of its own, starting as it did as part of a theater piece in a small East Village theater and then moving further out and into the world until it inspired the founding of the The Trevor Project. But the truth is so many have made this story happen and I'd like to acknowledge some of them here.

I want to thank all those amazing people of the theater who helped me develop *Trevor* by providing me with a stage: Randy Rollison at HERE Arts Center in New York, Mitchell Riggs at Camilla's, and the legendary Ellen Stewart at La Mama Etc.; Eve Ensler for her profound devotion to the work, for teaching me what theater is capable of, and for being my sister; Julian Schlossberg, Elaine May, and Mike Nichols for their incredible support and for providing me with a wider audience; and Cy O'Neal for always believing in me and championing my cause.

I want to thank Randy Stone and Peggy Rajski for having the vision that the little story of *Trevor* could become a film. Their dedication and hard work allowed me to believe that there is no dream too big. Blessings to Jodie Foster for her generosity with the start-up funds to make the film. And my heartfelt thanks to Diane Wade who was there at the very beginning to make it all happen, and who continues to support The Trevor Project with her untiring efforts.

I am so grateful to Brett Barsky for bringing the character of Trevor so beautifully to life, and to his mom, Cheryl Astroff. Without Cheryl's courageous and generous heart, her thirteen-year-old son would never have found his way to us.

I want to thank HBO and Ellen Degeneres for their support of the film and for helping us get into the homes of a whole generation of LGBT and Questioning teens and at a time when the word "gay" was only just beginning to be spoken on TV.

I want to thank my amazing agent and friend, Bill Clegg, for always respecting me and fighting for me—and for coming up with the brilliant idea of turning the story of *Trevor* into a book for a new generation of LGBT and Questioning teens. Dan Simon and Crystal Yakacki at Seven Stories Press, for realizing this idea so perfectly and with such care.

Thank you to my wild tribe of brothers and sisters;

these are the people who encourage me with their lives and through their work: Amy Bloom, Melanie Braverman, Matt Burgess, Dustin Lance Black, David Cafiero, Kate Clinton, Ken Corbett, Michael Cunningham, Jimmy Davis, Stacey D'Erasmo, Michael Downing, Tom Duane, Joy Episalla, Chris Garneau, Meg Giles, Brad Goreski, Tim Hailand, David Hopson, Jim Hodges, Gary Janetti, Daniel Kaizer, Michael Klein, Mark Matousek, Armistead Maupin, Christian McCulloch, Ian McKellen, Hilla Medalia, Marty Moran, Adam Moss, Christopher Potter, Beth Povinelli, Dave Purcell, Mollie Purdue, Seth Pybas, Sal Randolph, Randy Redd, Duncan Sheik, Christopher Turner, Lorraine Whittington, and Carrie Yamaoka.

A special thanks to Sally Fisher and Jim Rogers of the Colin Higgins Foundation who provided us with the start-up money to begin The Trevor Project back in 1998 and who have stood by us ever since.

And my deepest gratitude to every lifeline counselor who ever answered a call from a kid in crisis; they are the true heroes of this story.

RESOURCE GUIDE

NATIONAL ORGANIZATIONS

**Gay & Lesbian Alliance
Against Defamation (GLAAD)**
5455 Wilshire Boulevard
Los Angeles, CA 90036
http://www.glaad.org/

GSA Network
1550 Bryant Street, #800
San Francisco, CA 94103
http://gsanetwork.org/

Gay and Lesbian Medical Association (GLMA)
1326 18th Street, NW, Suite 22
Washington, DC 20036
http://www.glma.org/

Human Rights Campaign (HRC)
1640 Rhode Island Avenue NW
Washington, DC 20036
http://www.hrc.org/

National Center for Transgender Equality
1325 Massachusetts Avenue, NW, #700
Washington, DC 20005
http://transequality.org/

**Parents, Families and Friends of
Lesbians and Gays (PFLAG)**
1828 L Street NW, #660
Washington, DC 20036
www.pflag.org/

The Trevor Project
8704 Santa Monica Boulevard, Suite 200
West Hollywood, CA 90069
http://www.thetrevorproject.org/

TransYouth Family Allies (TYFA)
PO Box 1471
Holland, MI 49422
http://imatyfa.org/

American Civil Liberties Union (ACLU)
125 Broad Street, 18th Floor
New York, NY 10004
http://www.aclu.org/

Gay, Lesbian & Straight Education Network (GLSEN)
90 Broad Street
New York, NY 10004
www.glsen.org/

Lambda Legal
120 Wall Street, 19th Floor
New York, NY 10005
www.lambdalegal.org/

National Gay and Lesbian Taskforce (NGLTF)
1325 Massachusetts Avenue, NW, #600
Washington, DC 20005
http://thetaskforce.org/

WEBSITES

Advocates for Youth
www.advocatesforyouth.org

Amplify
www.amplifyyourvoice.org/youthresource

GLBT Near Me
www.glbtnearme.com

Go Ask Alice
www.goaskalice.columbia.edu

It Gets Better
http://www.itgetsbetter.org/

Lesbian, Gay, Bisexual and Transgender Health, CDC
www.cdc.gov/lgbthealth

Scarleteen
www.scarleteen.com

TrevorSpace
www.trevorspace.org

CRISIS INTERVENTION & SUICIDE PREVENTION LIFELINES

The Trevor Lifeline
866-4-U-Trevor (866-488-7386)

National Suicide Prevention Lifeline
800-273-TALK (8255)

THE TREVOR PROJECT

*E*ach one of us deserves a chance to dream of the future, no matter who we love or how we express our gender. The Trevor Project is here for young lesbian, gay, bisexual, transgender, queer, and questioning people to help whenever you or a friend might need to talk to someone. Through our lifesaving programs and information, we work every day to help make the future better for all LGBTQ youth.

The Trevor Project operates the 24-hour Trevor Lifeline, and also the TrevorChat online messaging service, both connecting young LGBTQ people to open and accepting counselors, free of charge. Plus, there is TrevorSpace.org, where thousands of young LGBTQ people from all over the world can connect in a safe and accepting social space. Trevor is also on Facebook, Twitter, and YouTube, connecting young people with positive messages every day.

If you or someone you care about feels depressed or is considering taking their own life, please call The Trevor Lifeline at: 866-488-7386. The call is free and confidential. Visit TheTrevorProject.org to learn more.

ABOUT THE AUTHOR

JAMES LECESNE wrote the Academy Award–winning short film *Trevor*, which inspired the founding of The Trevor Project. He produced the documentary film *After the Storm*, which chronicles the struggles of a group of teens in New Orleans in the aftermath of Hurricane Katrina, and he founded the After the Storm Foundation. He has published two young adult novels, *Absolute Brightness* and *Virgin Territory*. An actor as well as a writer, James has appeared on TV, in film, and in the theater. His solo show *Word of Mouth* was awarded both a NY Drama Desk Award and an Outer Critics Circle Award, and his play, *The Road Home: Stories of the Children of War*, was presented at the International Peace Conference at The Hague.

ABOUT SEVEN STORIES PRESS

Seven Stories Press is an independent book publisher based in New York City. We publish works of the imagination by such writers as Nelson Algren, Russell Banks, Octavia E. Butler, Ani DiFranco, Assia Djebar, Ariel Dorfman, Coco Fusco, Barry Gifford, Hwang Sok-yong, Lee Stringer, and Kurt Vonnegut, to name a few, together with political titles by voices of conscience, including the Boston Women's Health Collective, Noam Chomsky, Angela Y. Davis, Human Rights Watch, Derrick Jensen, Ralph Nader, Loretta Napoleoni, Gary Null, Project Censored, Barbara Seaman, Alice Walker, Gary Webb, and Howard Zinn, among many others. Seven Stories Press believes publishers have a special responsibility to defend free speech and human rights, and to celebrate the gifts of the human imagination, wherever we can. For additional information, visit www.sevenstories.com.